MW00815516

THIS BOOK BELONGS TO:

Published By Engine 9 Studios

This book and characters are from the creative mind of the author and are meant to inspire imagination and adventure in all kids, young and old. This book was traditionally illustrated with watercolor and ink, on watercolor paper, with digital enhancements and editing. This is the first book in the Bartholomew Babbitt Series.
First Printed in 2018.

ISBN 978-0-692-15919-4
Published in the United States
Printed in China

Bartholomew Babbitt's Bathtime Bonanza

Written & Illustrated by Andrew J. Hall

To my son, my inspiration,

Asher Lee Orion- always keep your wild heart.

-AJH

Bartholomew Babbitt had a very bad habit
of taking a bath for hours and hours…

SOAP

He'd sit and he'd play
in the bubbles all day,
making a fantastical mess
in the most spectacular way.

“What is he doing?”
his mother would say.
“He's been in that tub
almost the whole entire day!”

"Oh, just let him be..." his father would utter
while eating some bread with jelly and butter.
But little did they know
the places he'd go
while taking his bath for
hours and hours.

Now there in the tub with bubbles aplenty
and the plethora of toys, who knows how many!
There were little green soldiers all up in a row,
with gray and blue sharks in the water below...

...A big rubber ducky tied up to a rope,
with bright-colored dinosaurs all stuck in the soap.
And caught in the waves but staying afloat
was a yellow and blue little tugboat.

When all of a sudden in no time at all,
Bartholomew Babbitt became ever so small.
The scream of the whistle and ding of the bell
and up from above the captain did yell!
“All hands on deck and anchors aweigh;
let's close up those hatches, we're well on our way!”

USS ORION

The water began churning
and the tugboat began turning
around and around as it circled the drain.

Then PLOOOP!
Down they went
as the tugboat was sent
on past the soap scum and mildewy stains.

They pushed through the hairballs that were ever so slimy.
And, oh! All that grease, boy was it grimy!

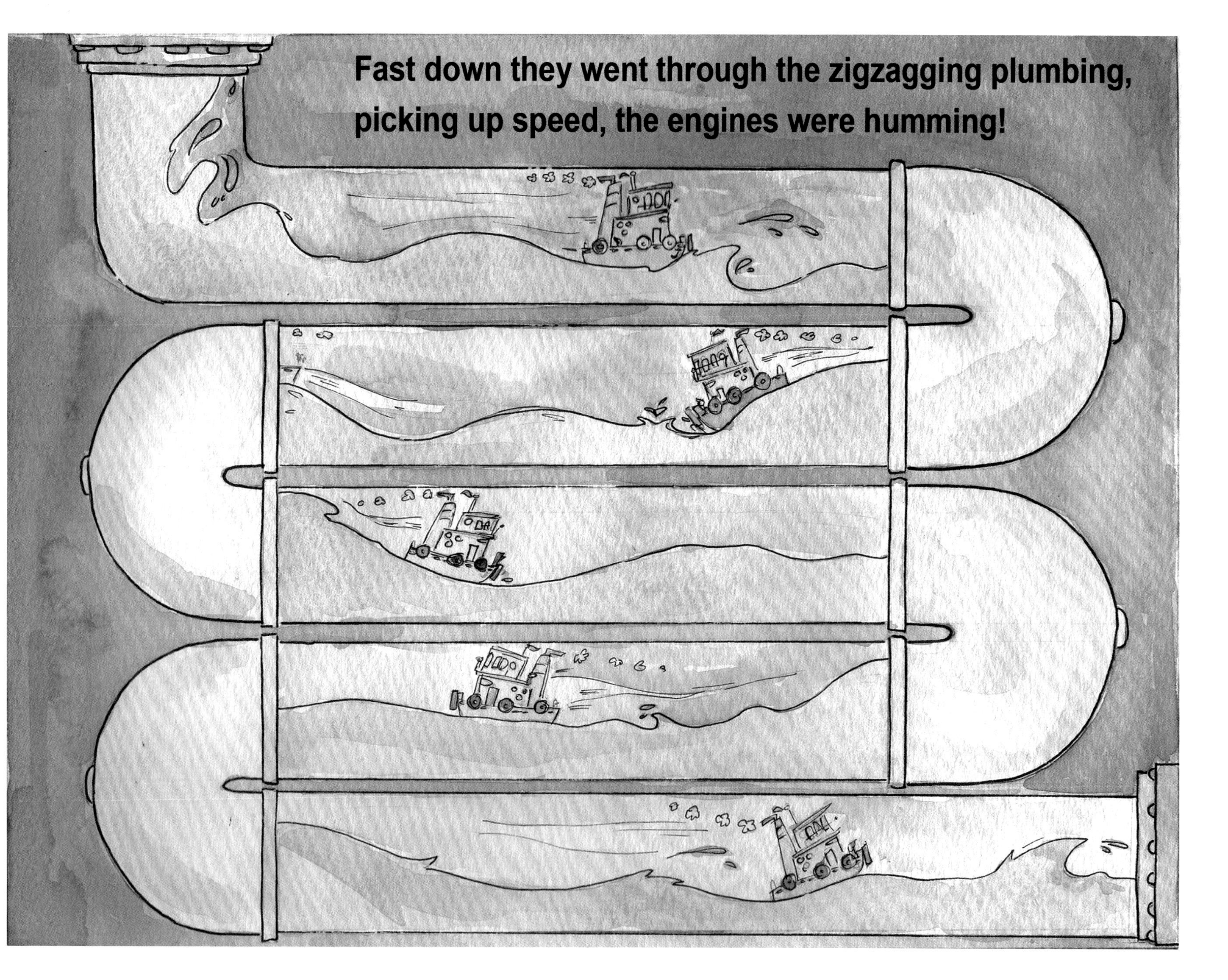
Fast down they went through the zigzagging plumbing,
picking up speed, the engines were humming!

Up and down and 'round they all went,
all through the city the tugboat was sent!

Crossing through tunnels
and zooming by trains,
passing by highways and flying by planes!

They came up through a hydrant and into a hose,
shot out of a nozzle and waved a hello!

Skipping along fountains in front of chateaus,
and back in the gutters to the sewers below.

The sewers were dark and a little bit dingy,
but wouldn't you know the folks were all friendly.
The family of mice were really quite nice,
and they got a big smile from the old crocodile.
The goldfish waved even though they'd been flushed
and the rat tipped his hat,
as the tugboat was rushed...

USS ORION
“...Onward, back home!” the cap'n said with delight.
“It's getting a bit late, it'll almost be night!”
Bartholomew grinned from the fun that had passed,
when “Ahoy!” yelled a sailor, from atop of the mast,
“I can see our return, it's coming in fast!”

H
C
Right through the faucet they came out in a dash,
back in the tub they made a big splash.
SPLASH!!!

There Bartholomew Babbitt waved his goodbyes,
and then he returned to his normal boy size.

Bedtime has now come with bathtime all done,
and his parents returned to tuck him in bed.
They wrapped him up right
and hugged him real tight
and gave him sweet kisses there on his head.

Now in his arms, the tugboat held tight,
he snuggled his pillow and said his good night,
and Bartholomew Babbitt grinned with delight
'cause of the fun in the tub from morning till night.

USS ORION
BON VOYAGE!!